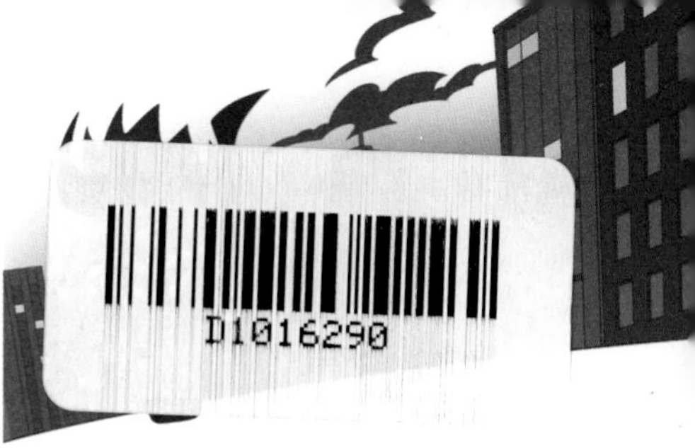

Dear Parents:

Congratulations! Your child is taking the first steps on an exciting journey. The destination? Independent reading!

STEP INTO READING® will help your child get there. The program offers five steps to reading success. Each step includes fun stories and colorful art or photographs. In addition to original fiction and books with favorite characters, there are Step into Reading Non-Fiction Readers, Phonics Readers and Boxed Sets, Sticker Readers, and Comic Readers—a complete literacy program with something to interest every child.

Learning to Read, Step by Step!

STEP 1

Ready to Read **Preschool–Kindergarten**
• **big type and easy words** • **rhyme and rhythm** • **picture clues**
For children who know the alphabet and are eager to begin reading.

STEP 2

Reading with Help **Preschool–Grade 1**
• **basic vocabulary** • **short sentences** • **simple stories**
For children who recognize familiar words and sound out new words with help.

STEP 3

Reading on Your Own **Grades 1–3**
• **engaging characters** • **easy-to-follow plots** • **popular topics**
For children who are ready to read on their own.

STEP 4

Reading Paragraphs **Grades 2–3**
• **challenging vocabulary** • **short paragraphs** • **exciting stories**
For newly independent readers who read simple sentences with confidence.

STEP 5

Ready for Chapters **Grades 2–4**
• **chapters** • **longer paragraphs** • **full-color art**
For children who want to take the plunge into chapter books but still like colorful pictures.

STEP INTO READING® is designed to give every child a successful reading experience. The grade levels are only guides; children will progress through the steps at their own speed, developing confidence in their reading.

Remember, a lifetime love of reading starts with a single step!

For Tanya and Ophelia
—C.W.

Copyright © 2017 DC Comics.
DC SUPER FRIENDS and all related characters and elements
© & ™ DC Comics.
WB SHIELD: ™ & © Warner Bros. Entertainment Inc. (s17)
RHUS38189

All rights reserved. Published in the United States by Random House Children's Books, a division of Penguin Random House LLC, 1745 Broadway, New York, NY 10019, and in Canada by Penguin Random House Canada Limited, Toronto.

Step into Reading, Random House, and the Random House colophon are registered trademarks of Penguin Random House LLC.

Visit us on the Web!
StepIntoReading.com
randomhousekids.com
dckids.kidswb.com

Educators and librarians, for a variety of teaching tools, visit us at RHTeachersLibrarians.com

ISBN 978-1-5247-1711-7 (trade) — ISBN 978-1-5247-1712-4 (lib. bdg.)
ISBN 978-1-5247-1713-1 (ebook)

Printed in the United States of America

10 9 8 7 6 5 4 3 2

STEP 2 READING WITH HELP

STEP INTO READING®

DC SUPER FRIENDS™

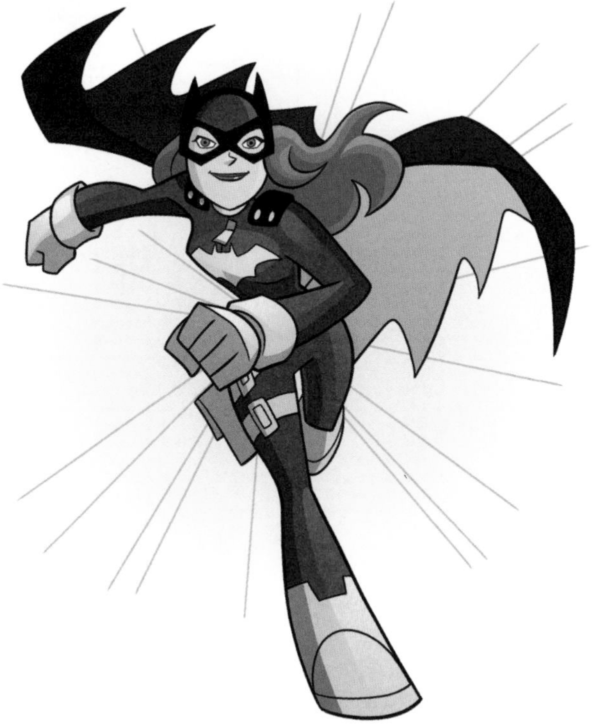

BRAVE BATGIRL!

by Christy Webster
illustrated by Erik Doescher

Random House New York

Meet Batgirl.

She is a super hero.

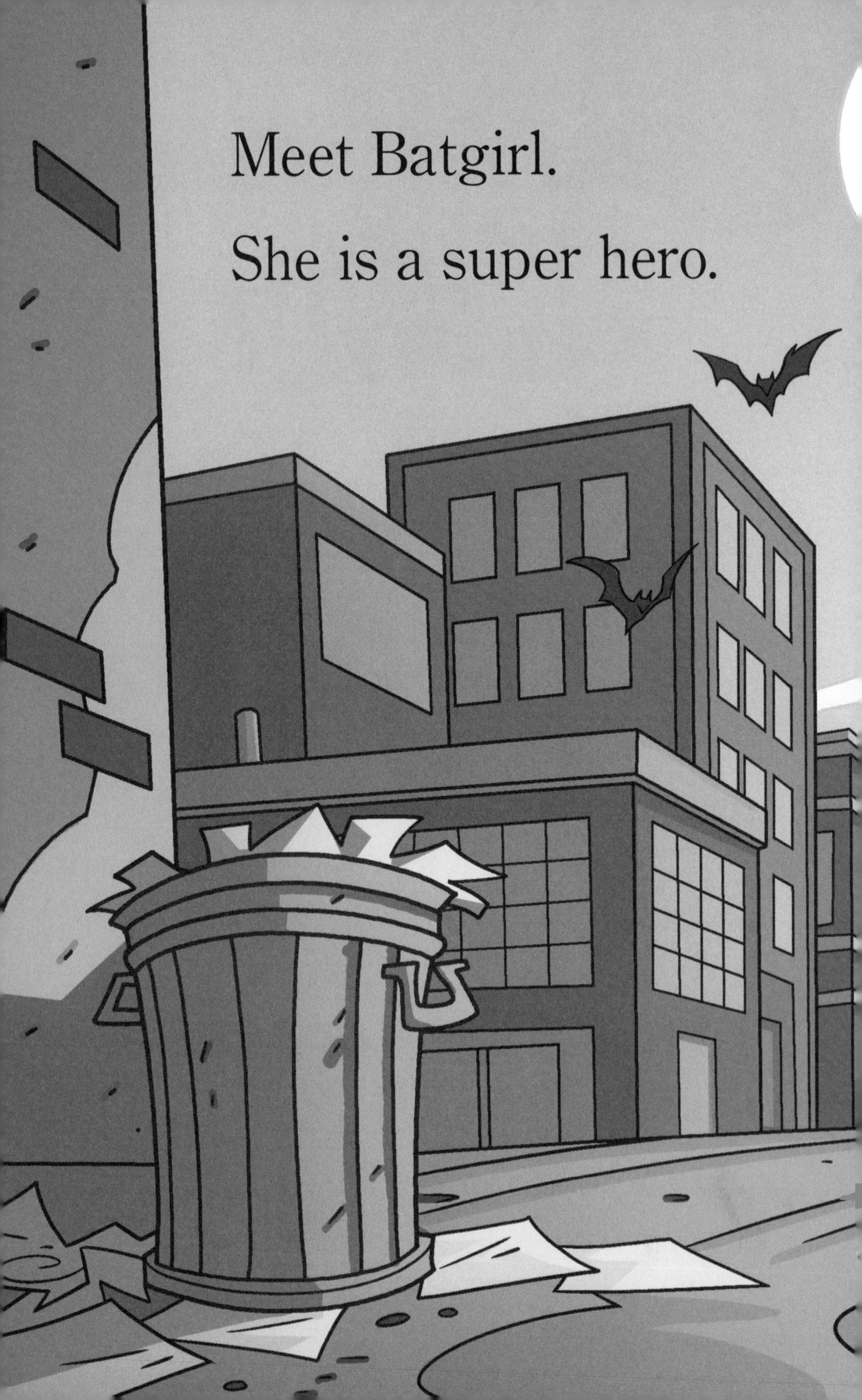

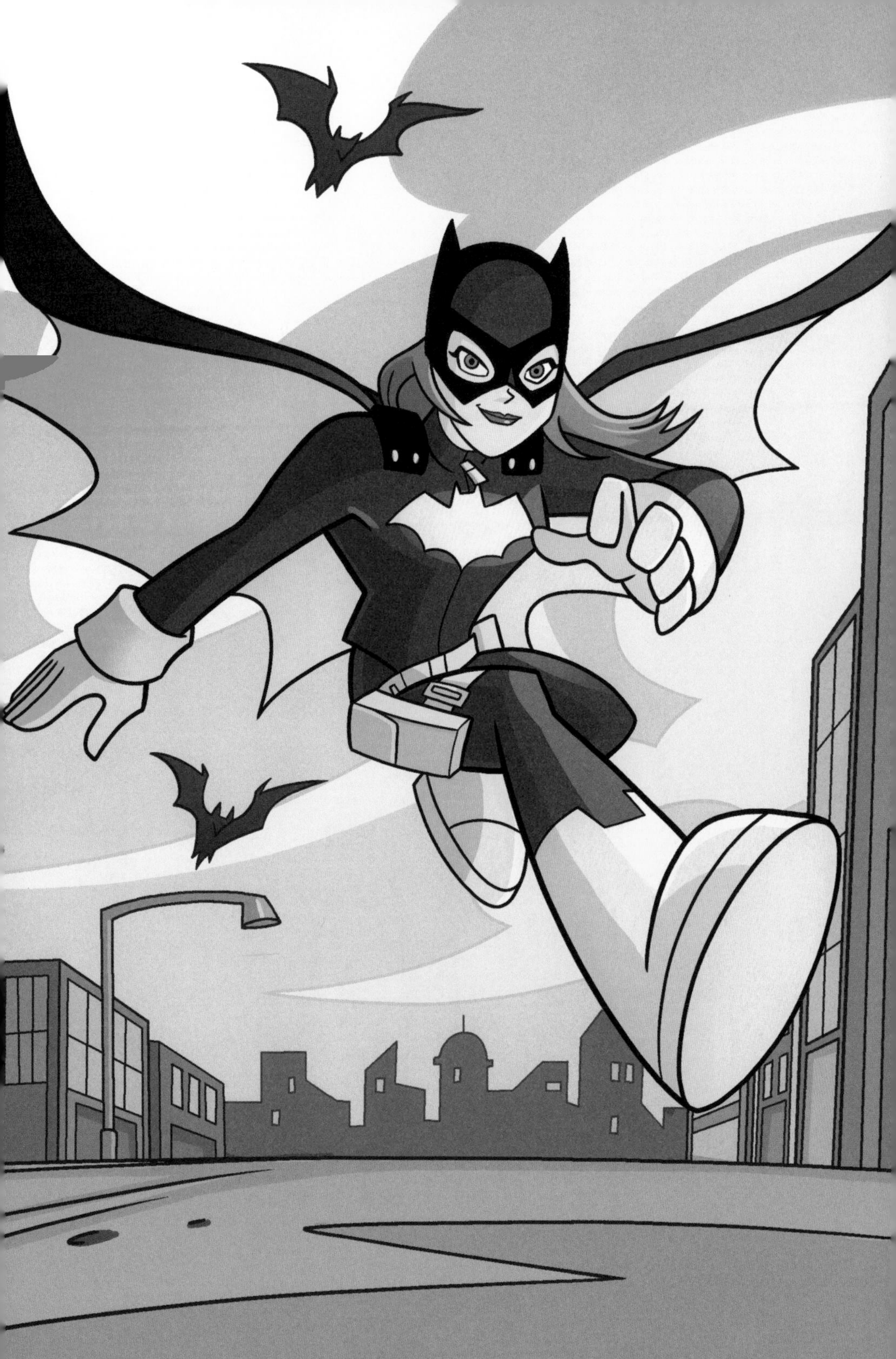

Batgirl lives
in Gotham City.

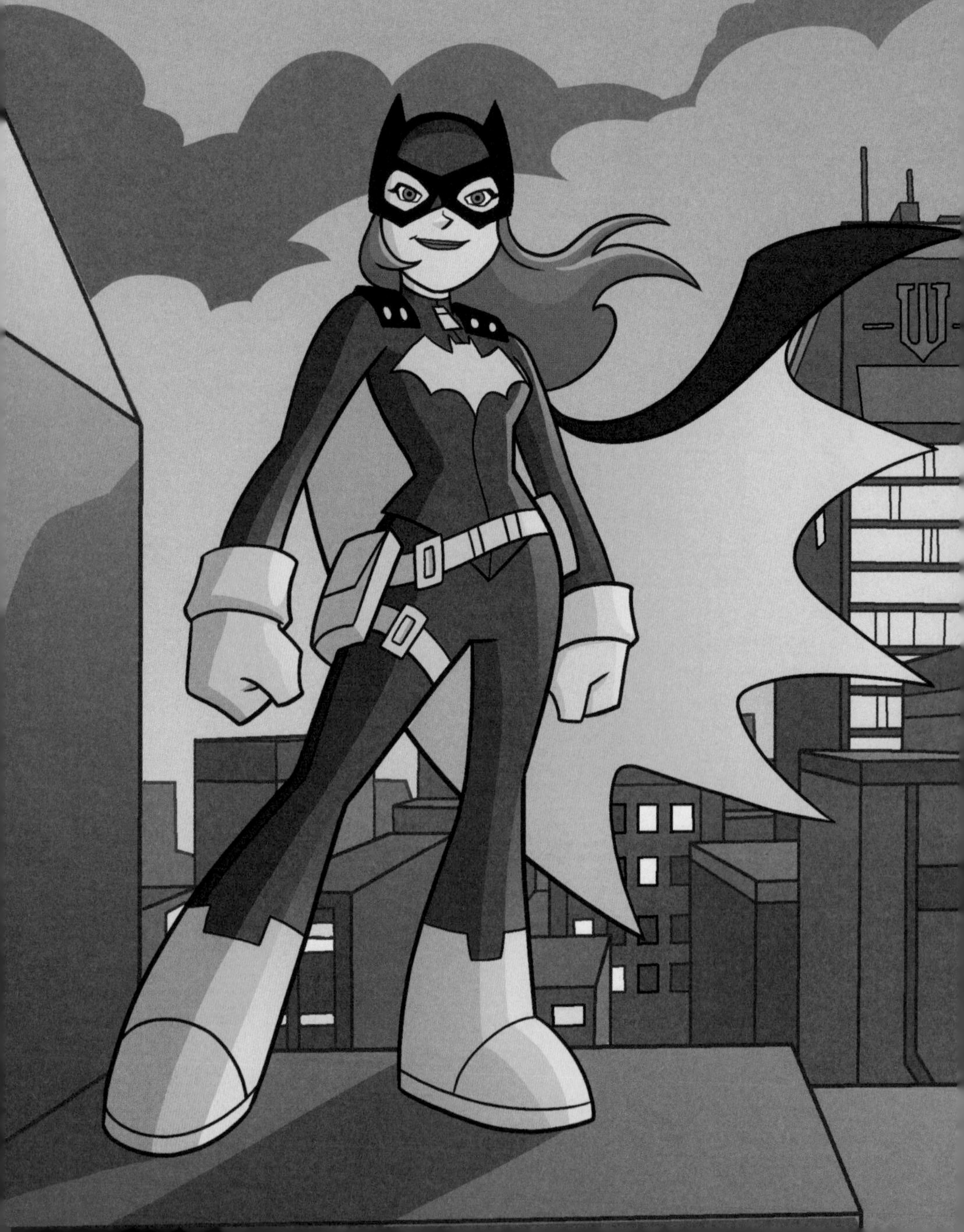

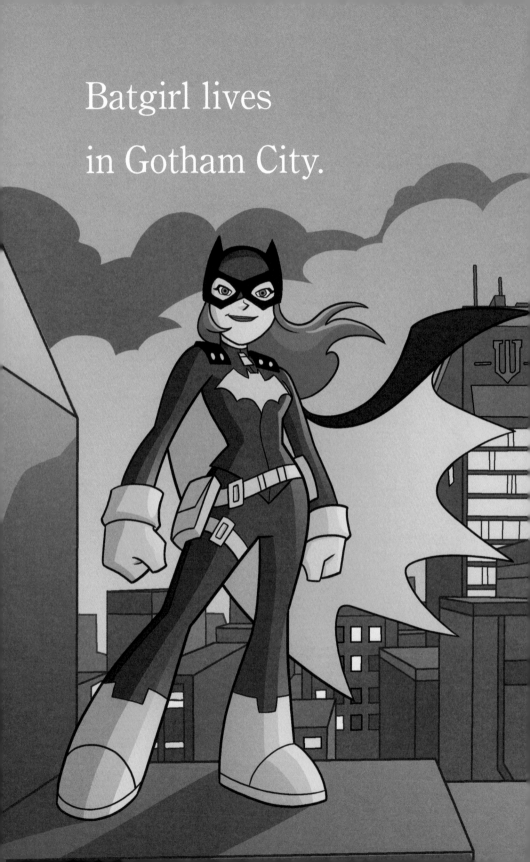

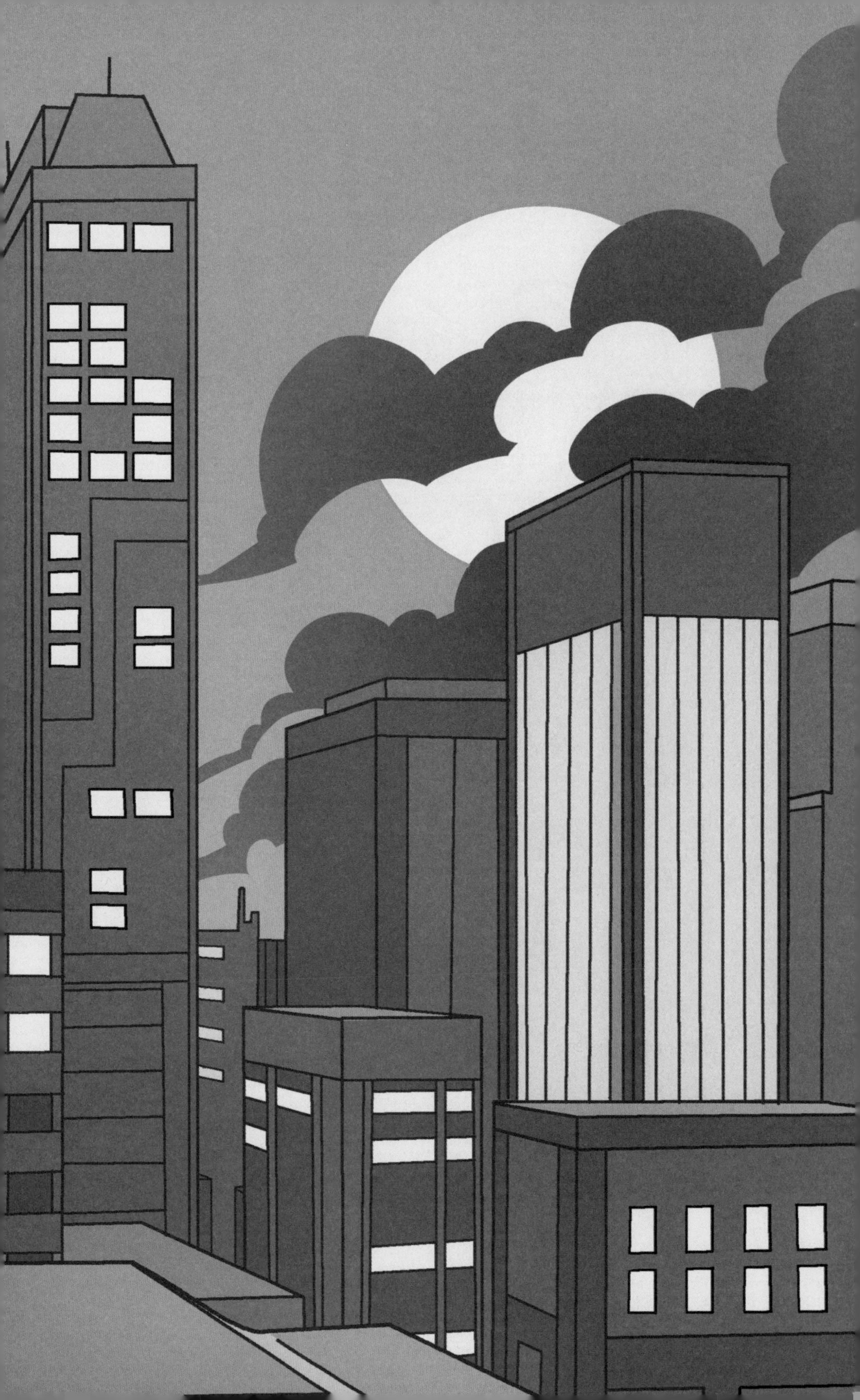

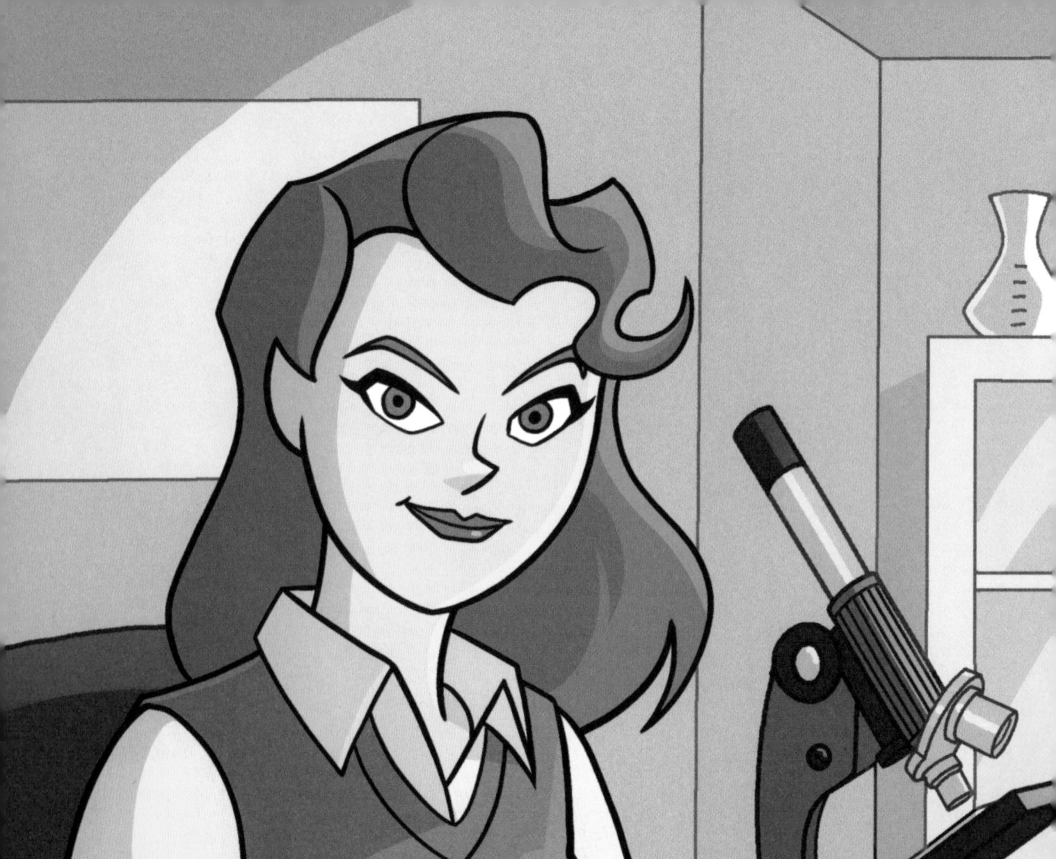

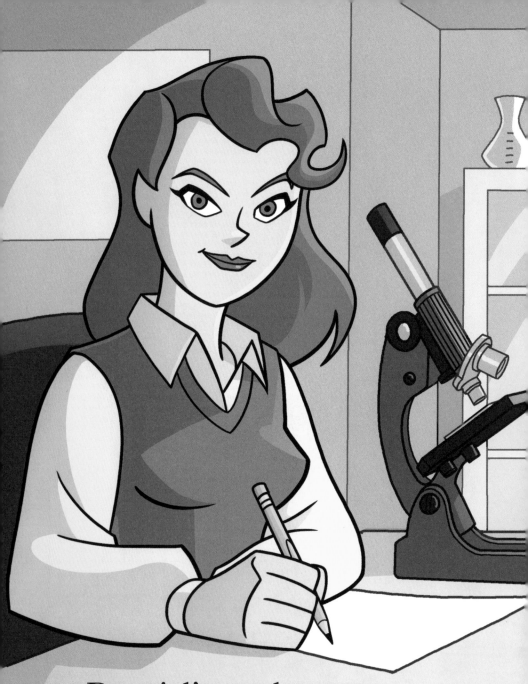

Batgirl's real name
is Barbara Gordon.

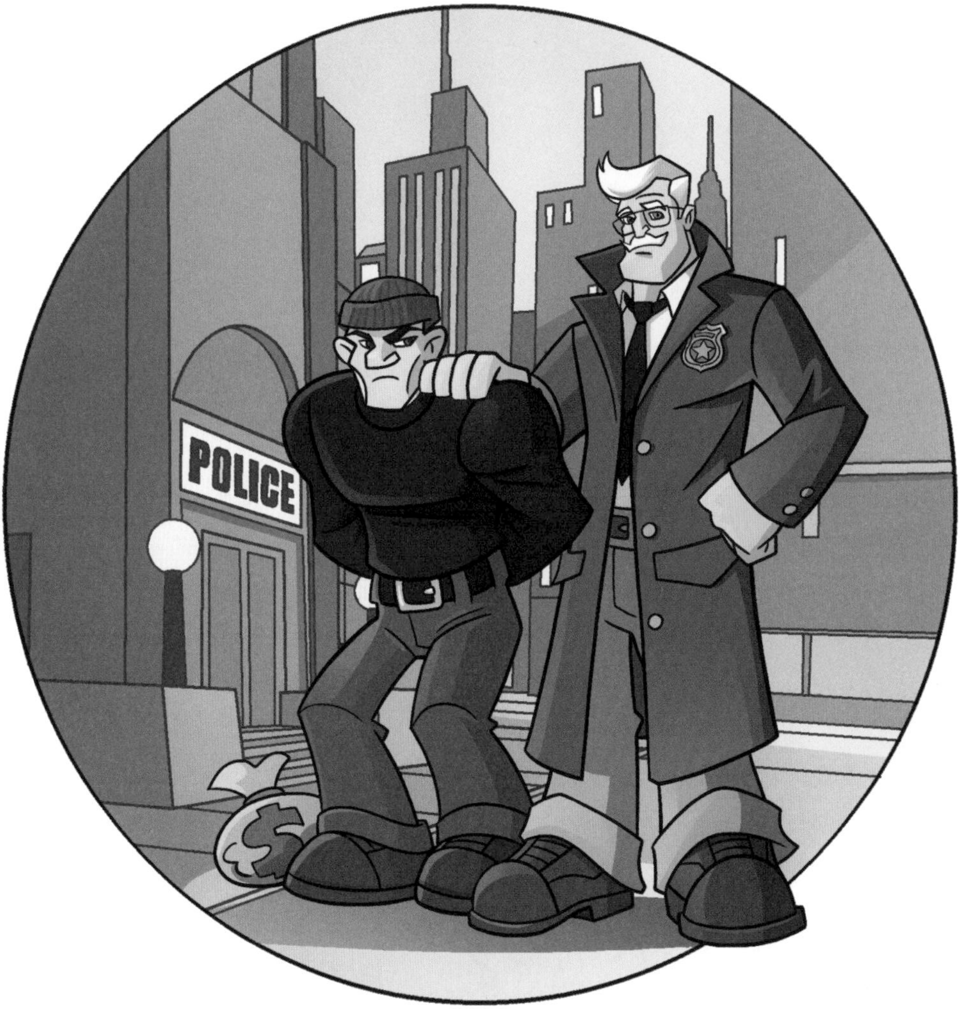
POLICE

Her father is

the police chief.

He fights crime.

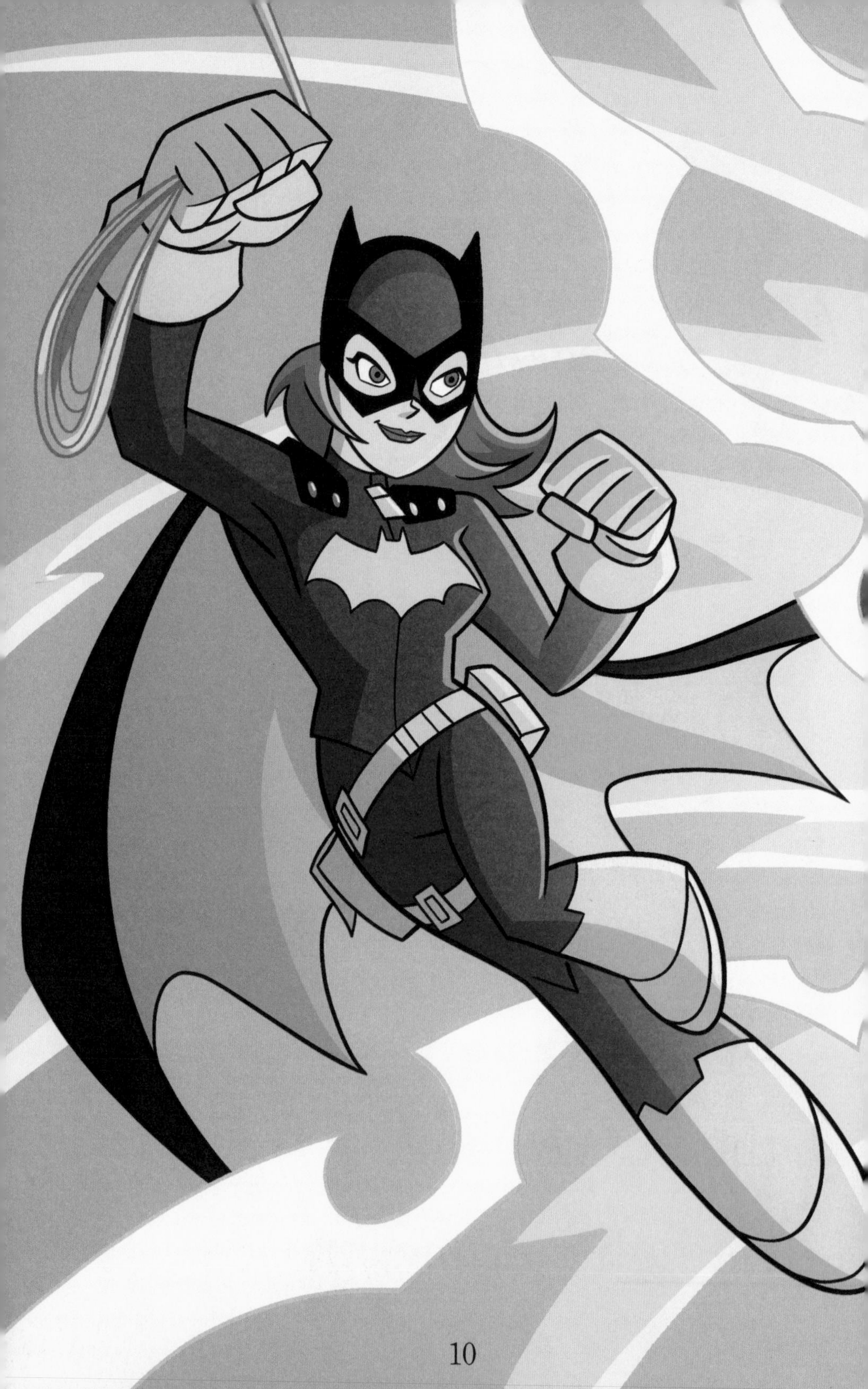

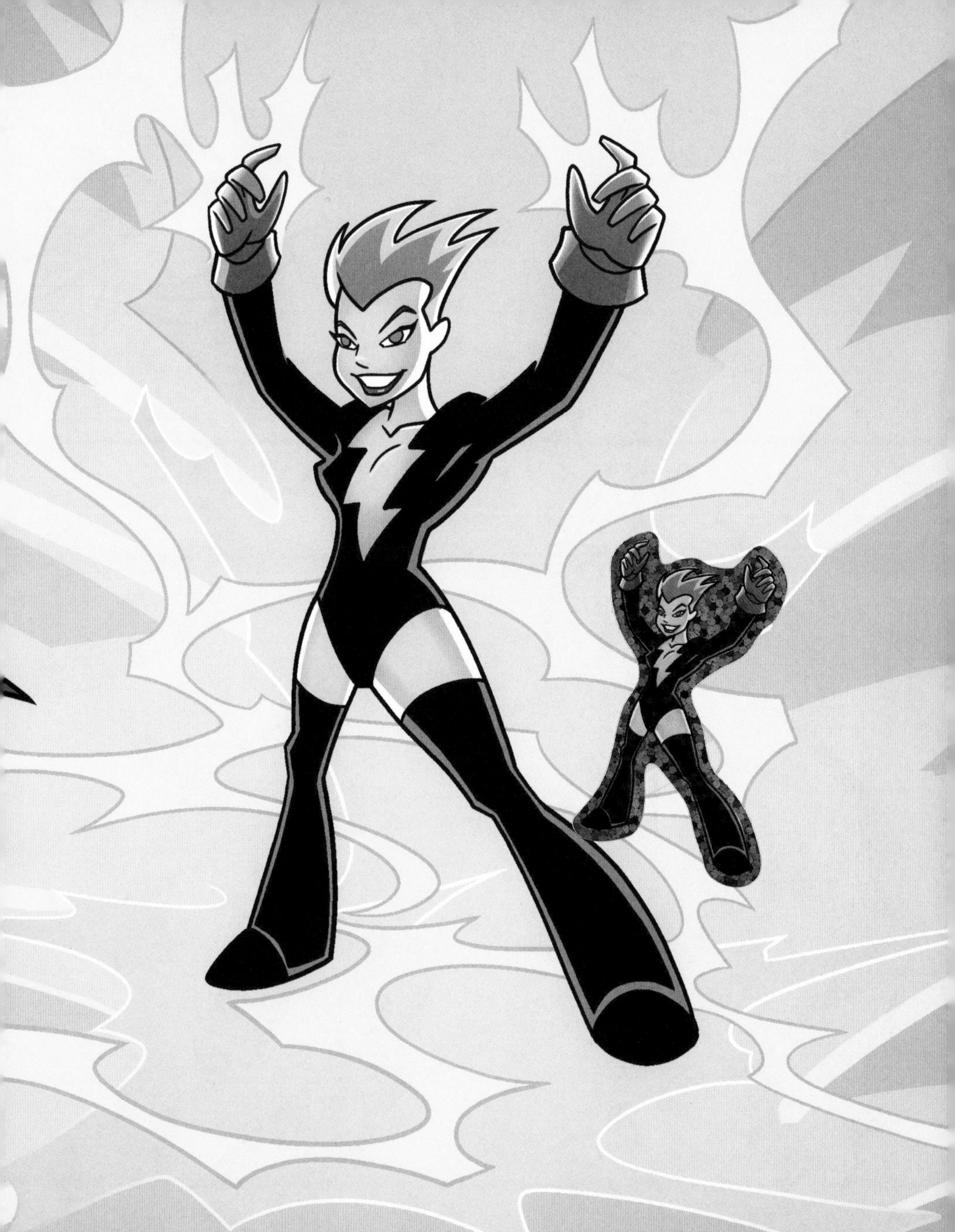

Batgirl fights crime, too.

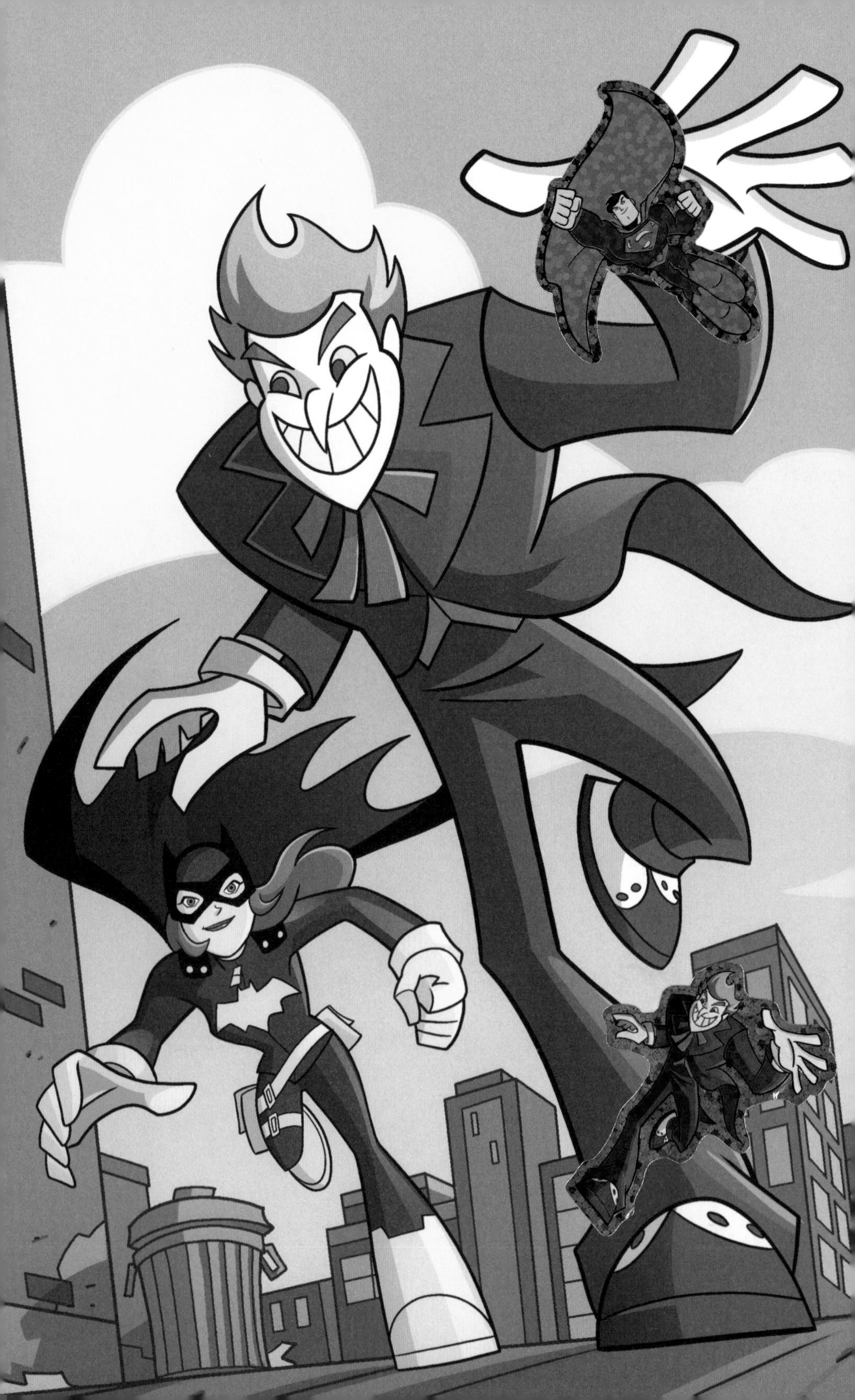

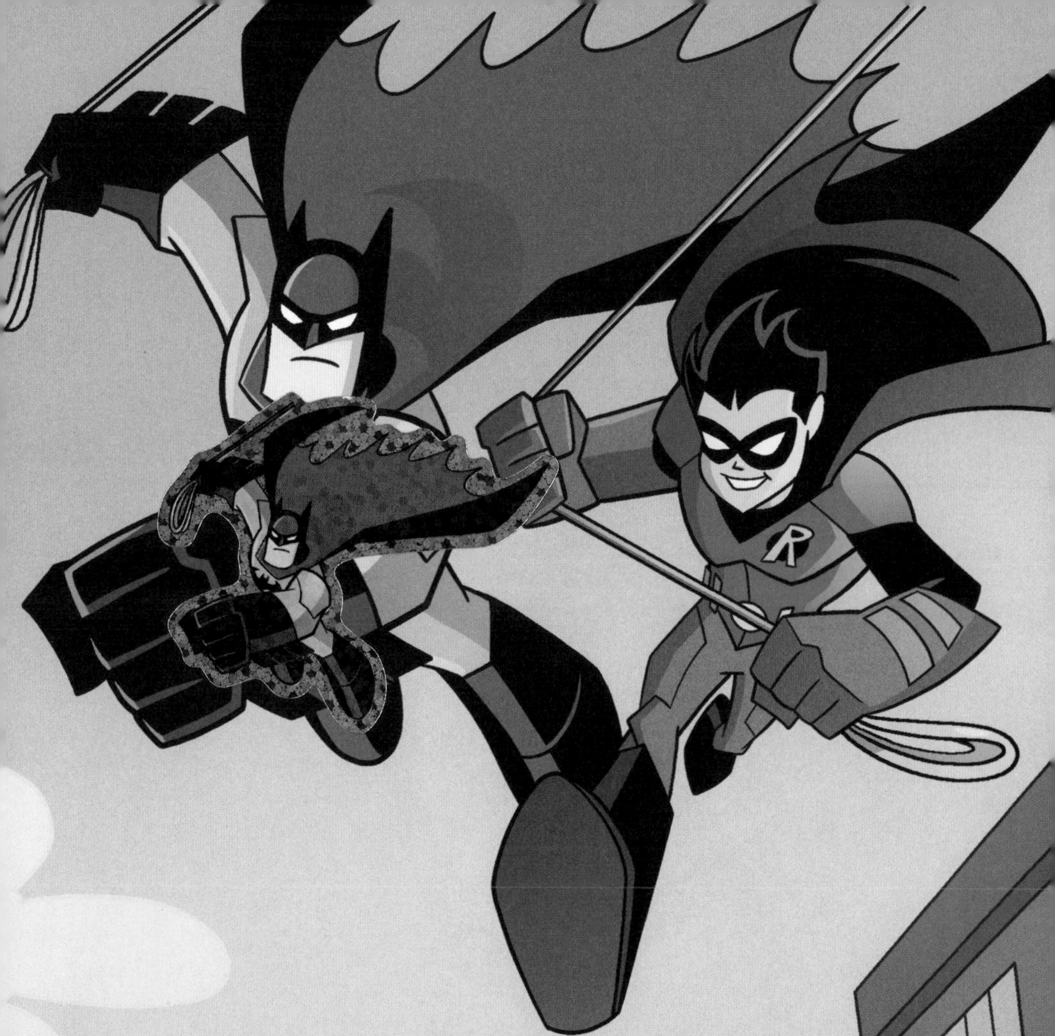

When trouble comes
to Gotham City,
Batgirl and her friends
race to the rescue!

Batgirl is smart.

She is a computer whiz.

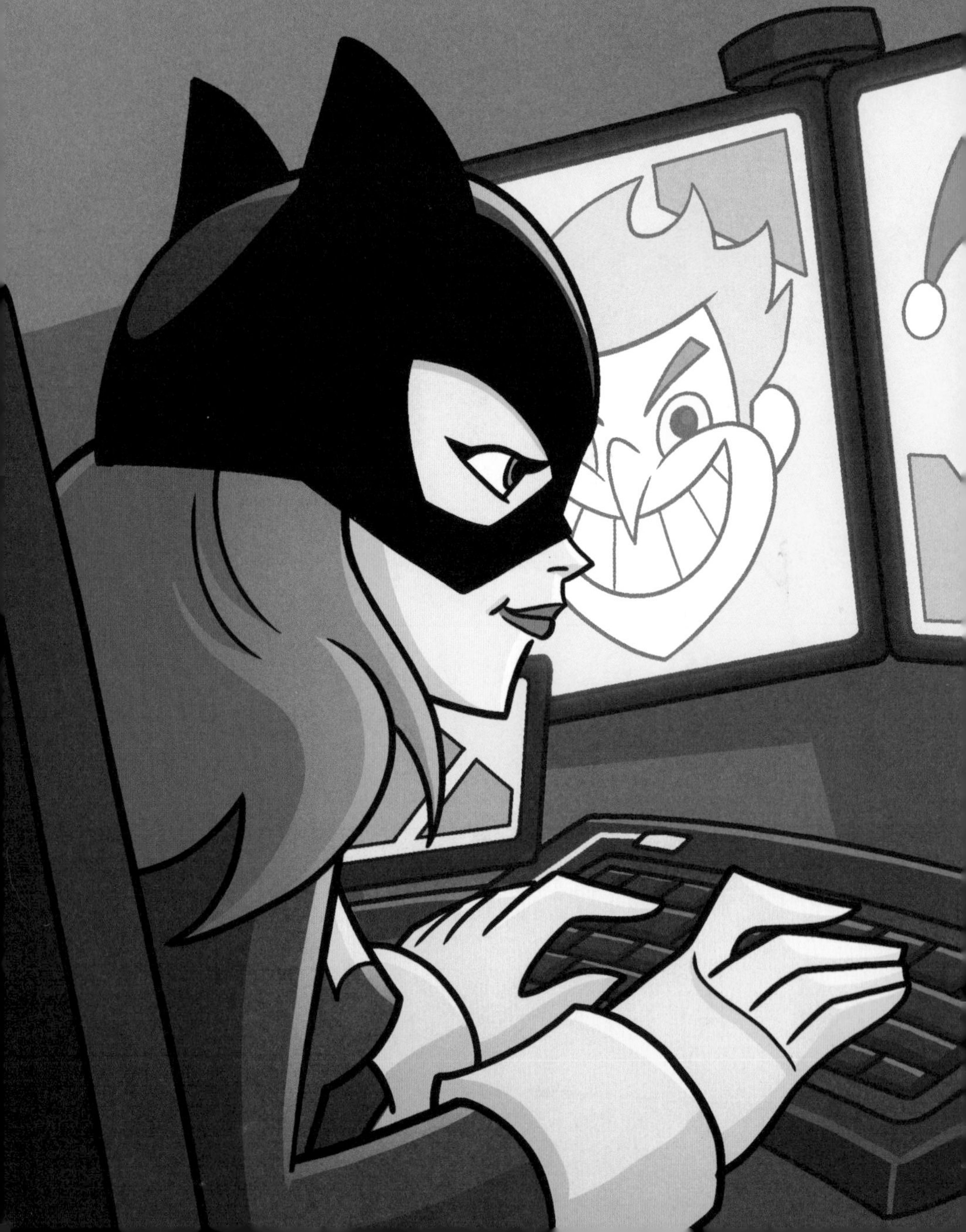

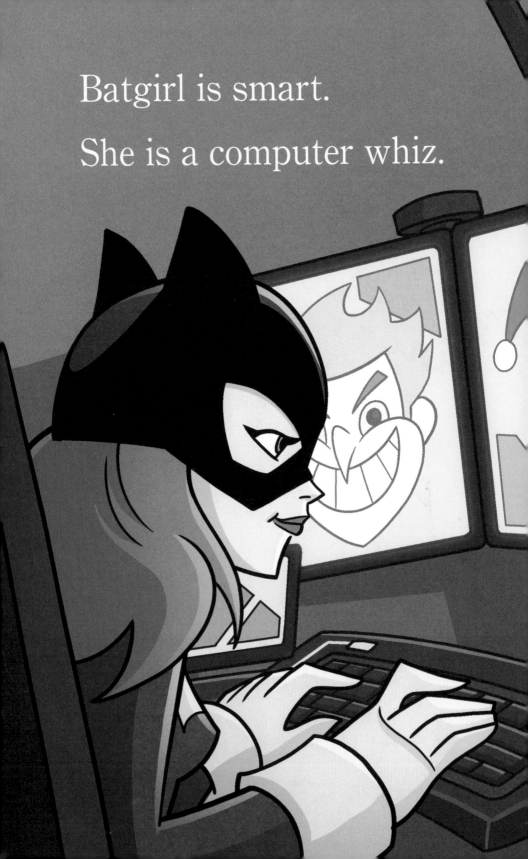

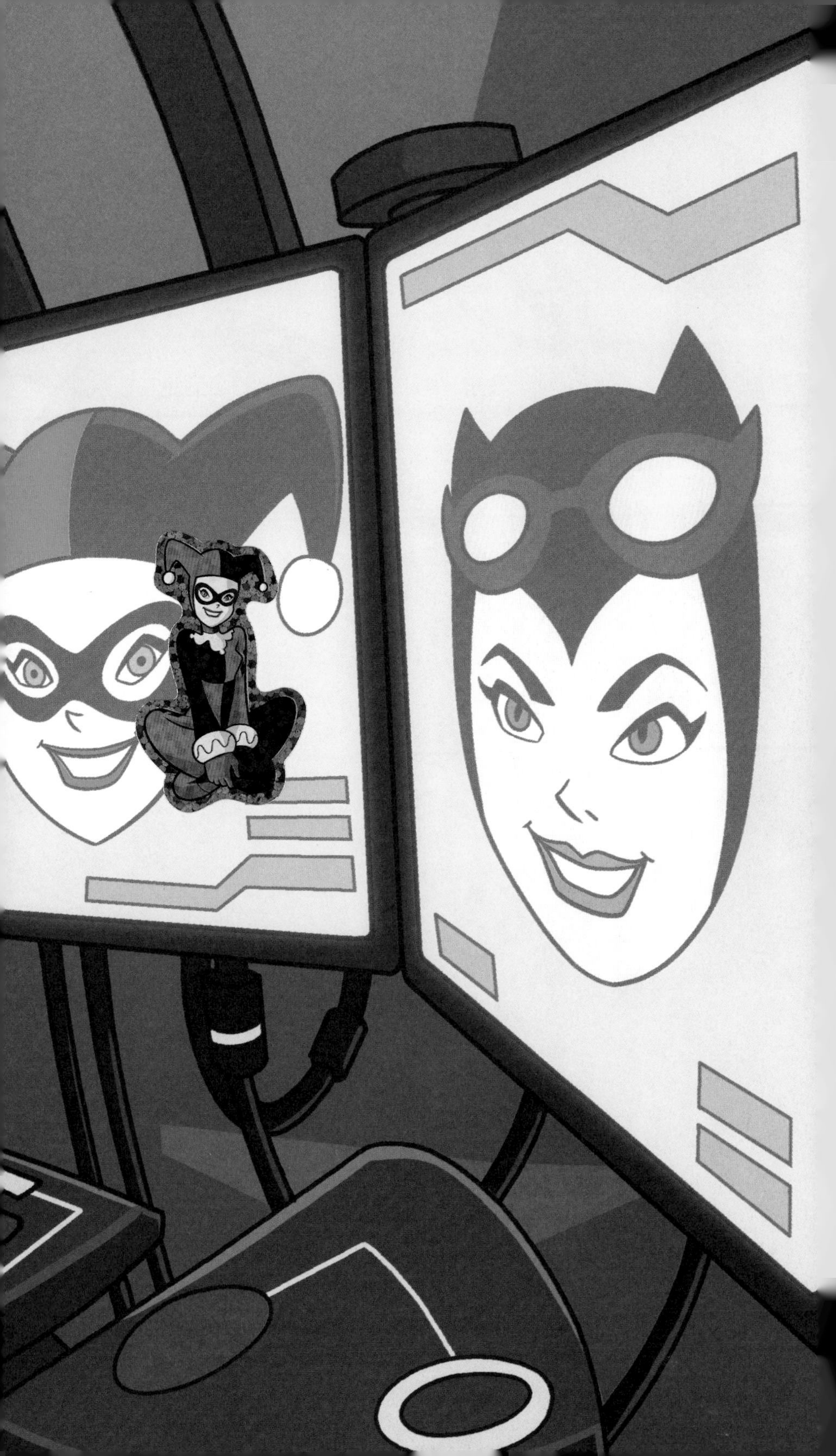

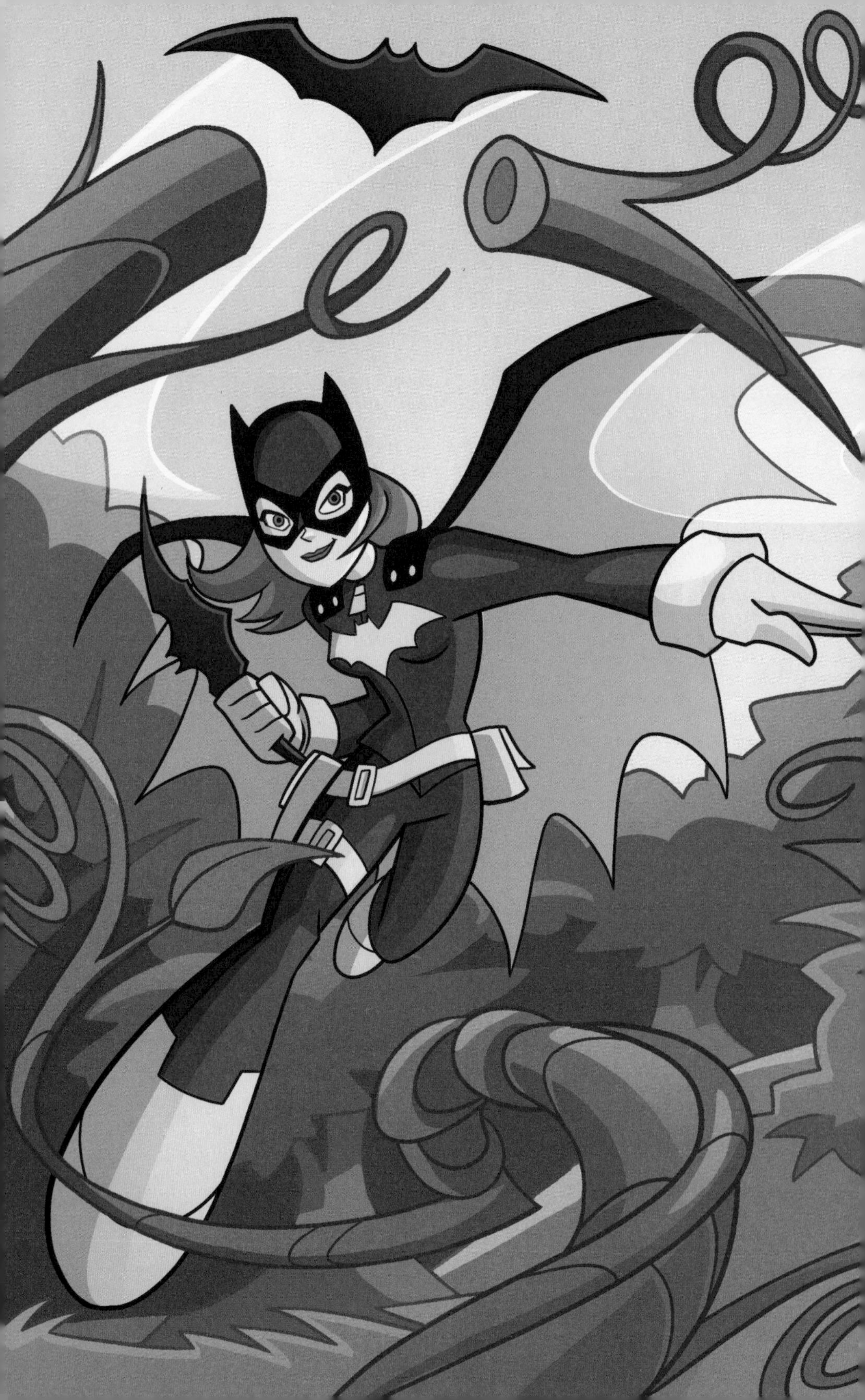

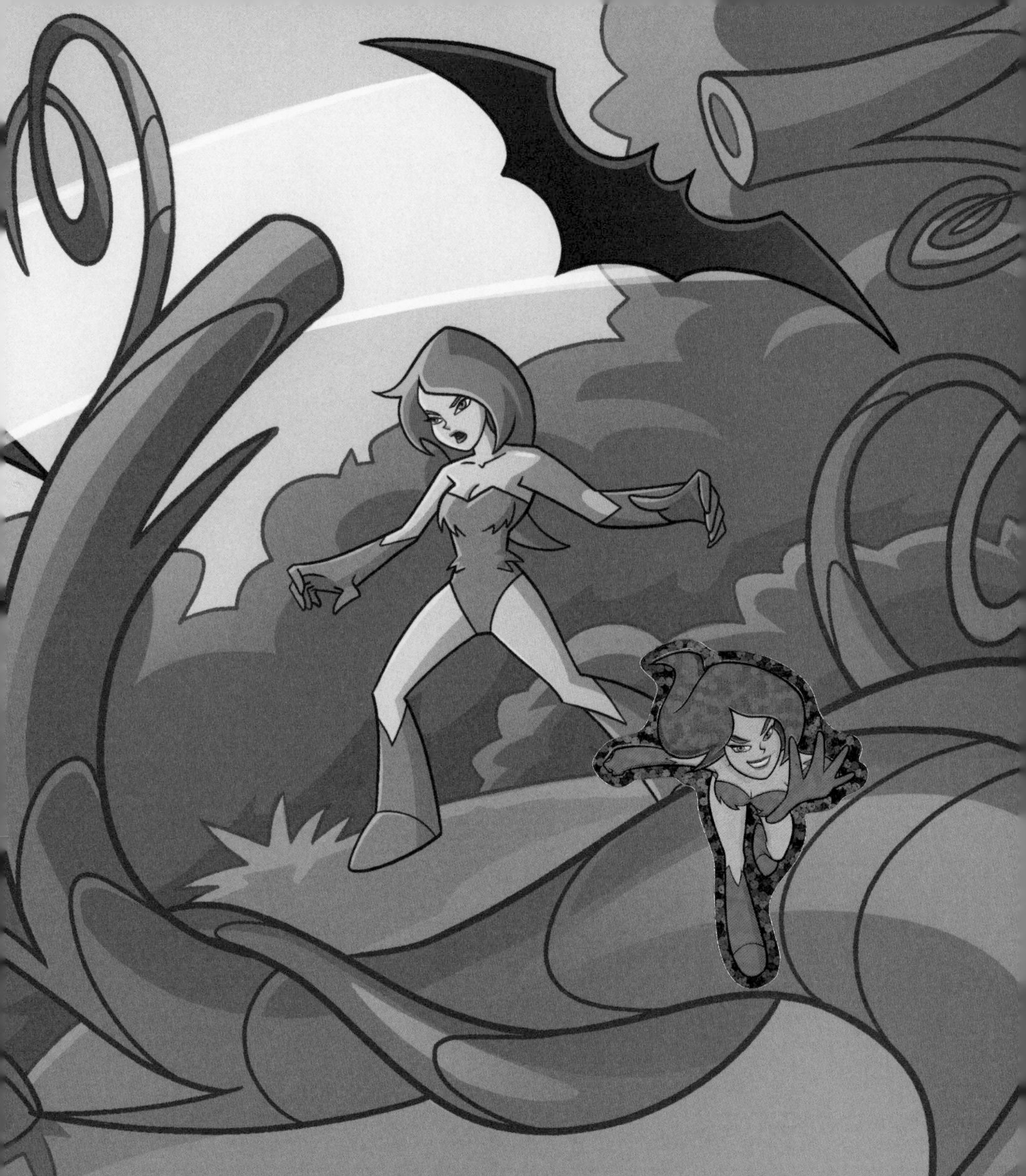

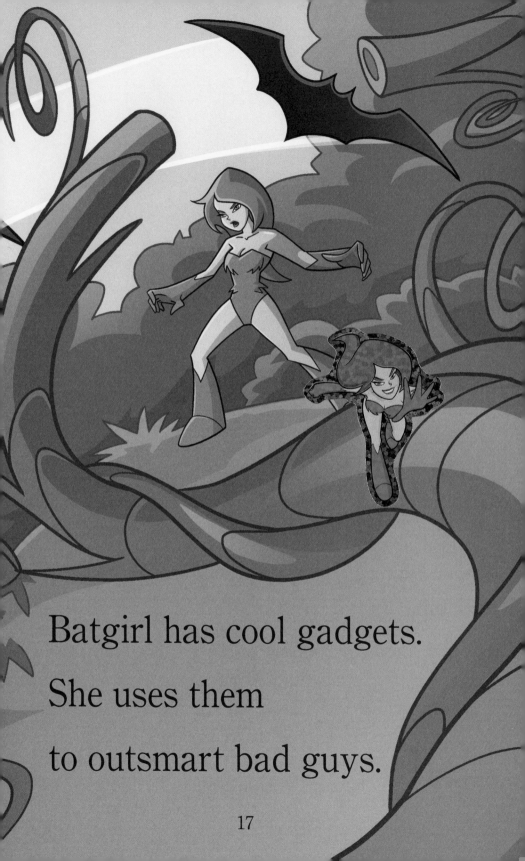

Batgirl has cool gadgets.
She uses them
to outsmart bad guys.

Batgirl is fast.

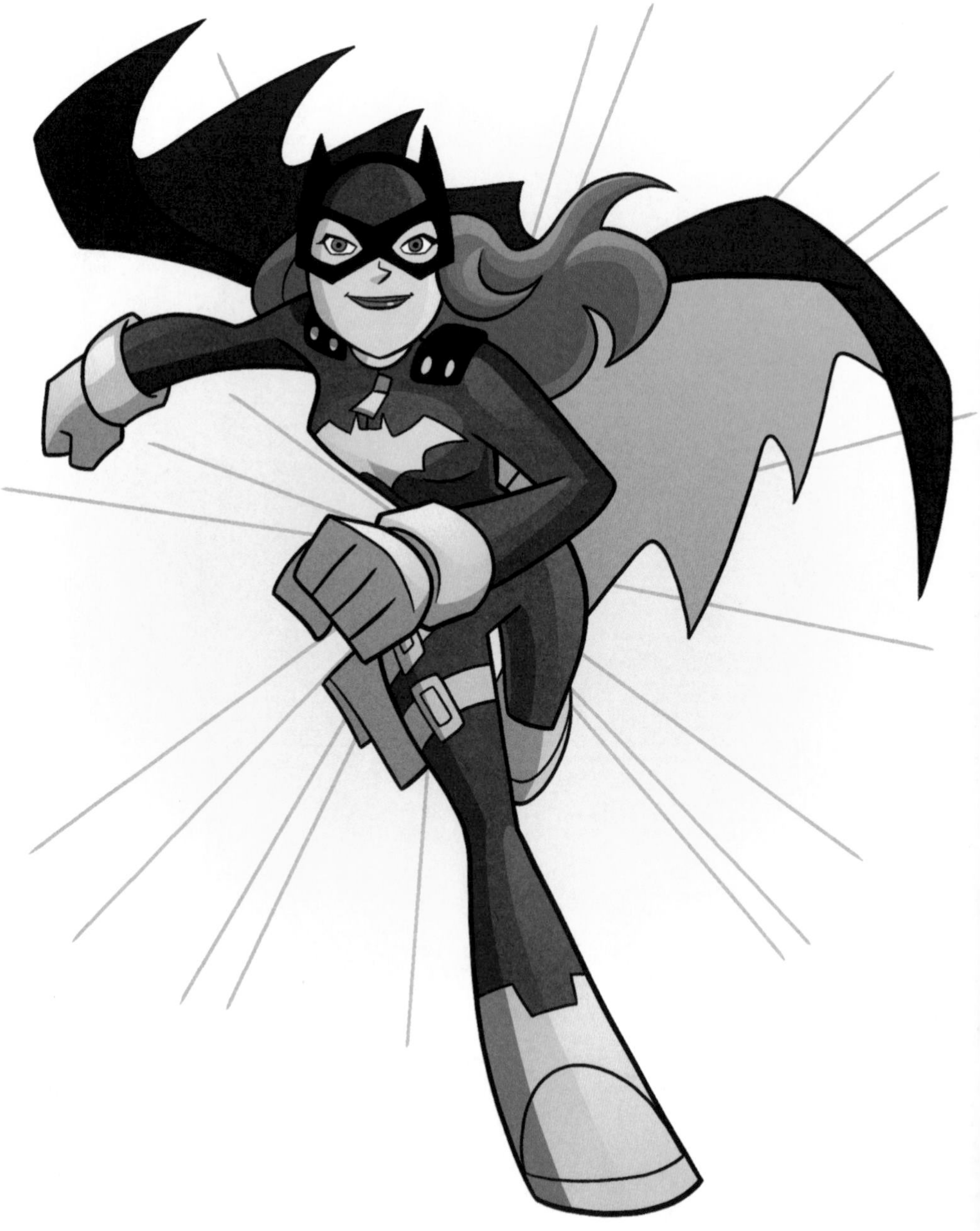

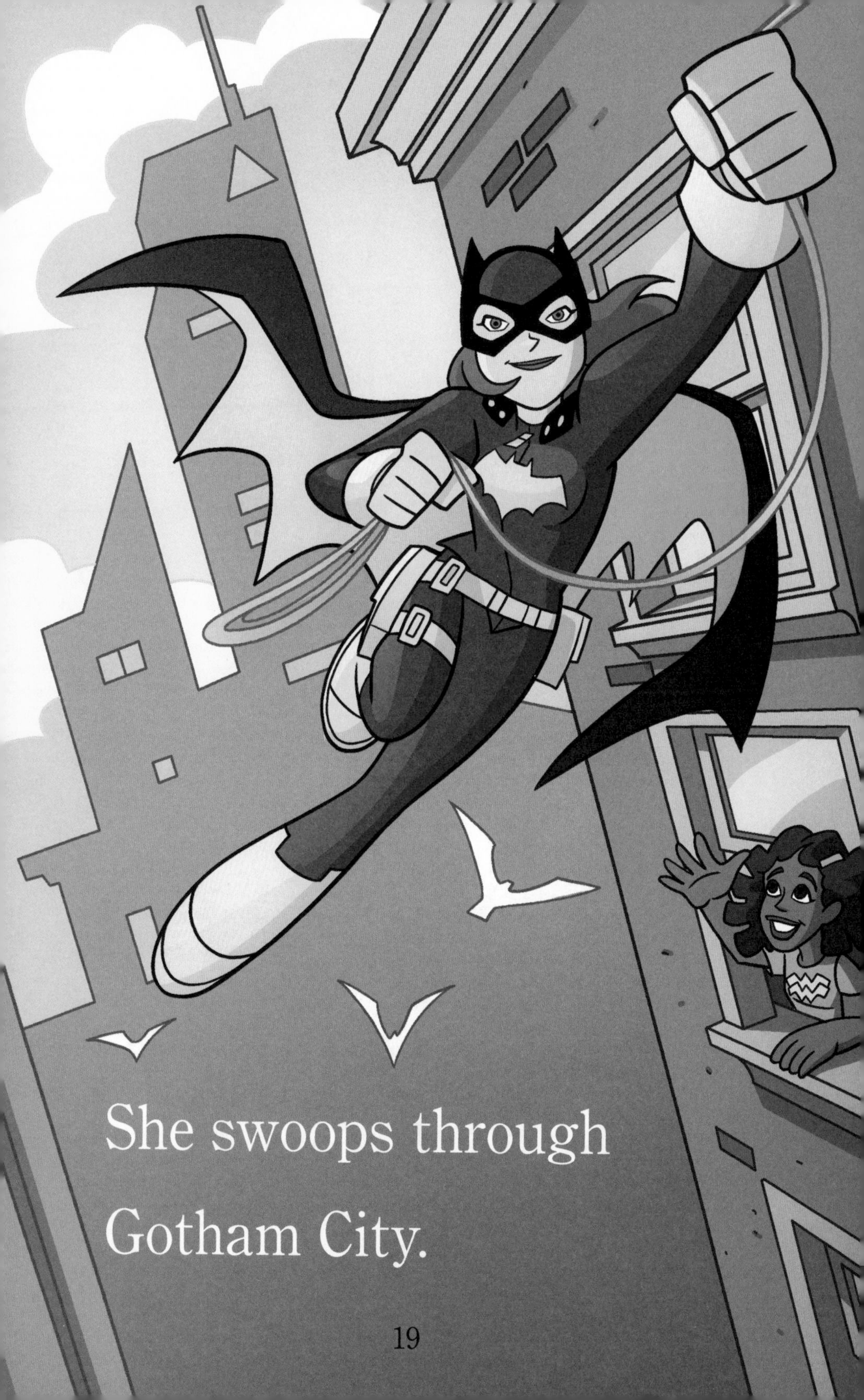

She swoops through
Gotham City.

She rides through

the streets.

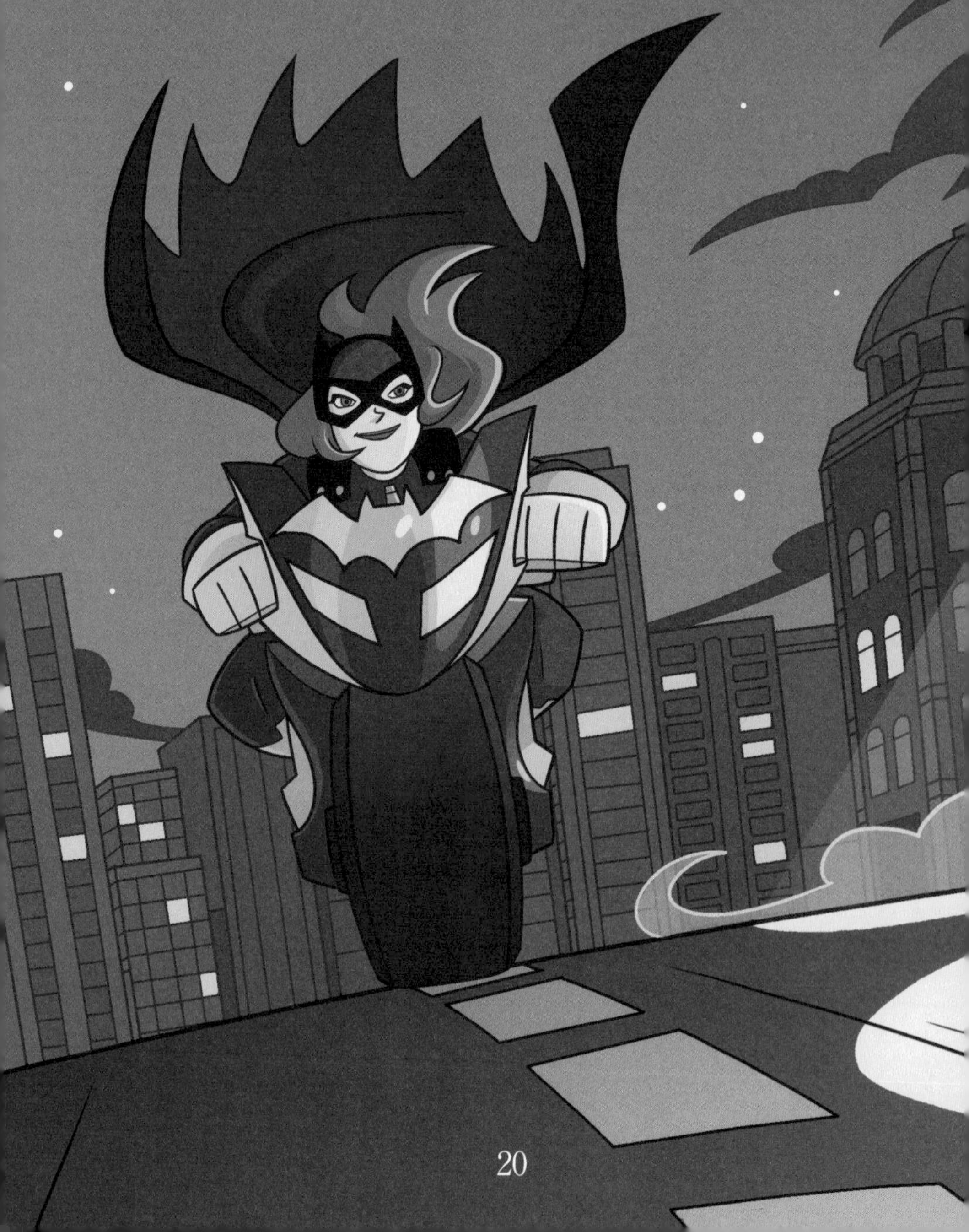

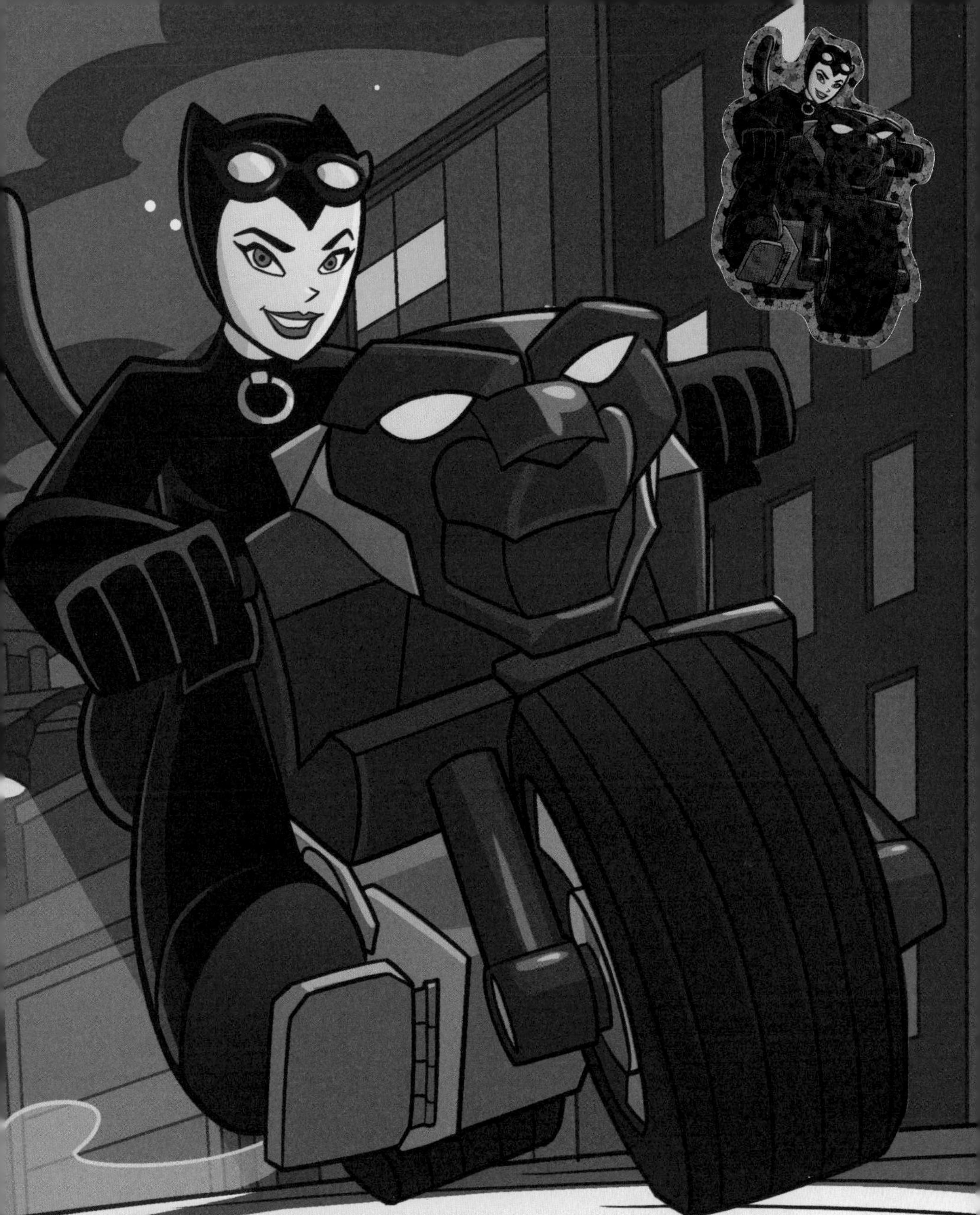

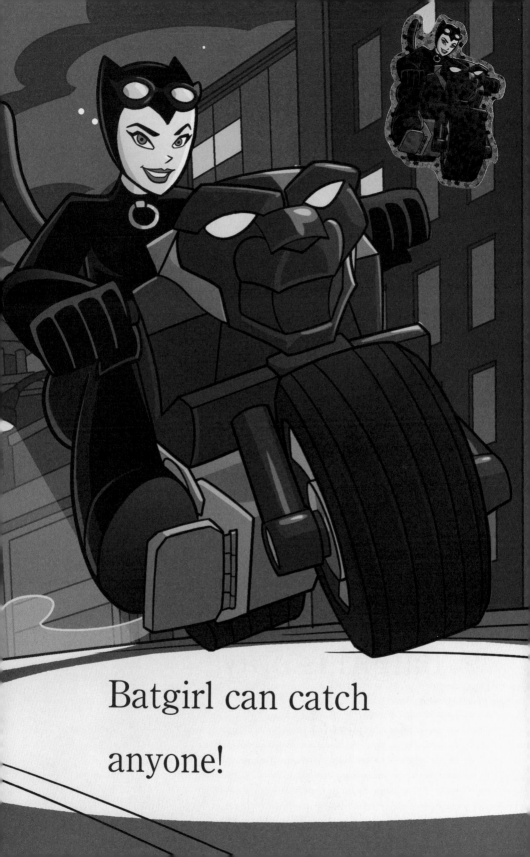

Batgirl can catch

anyone!

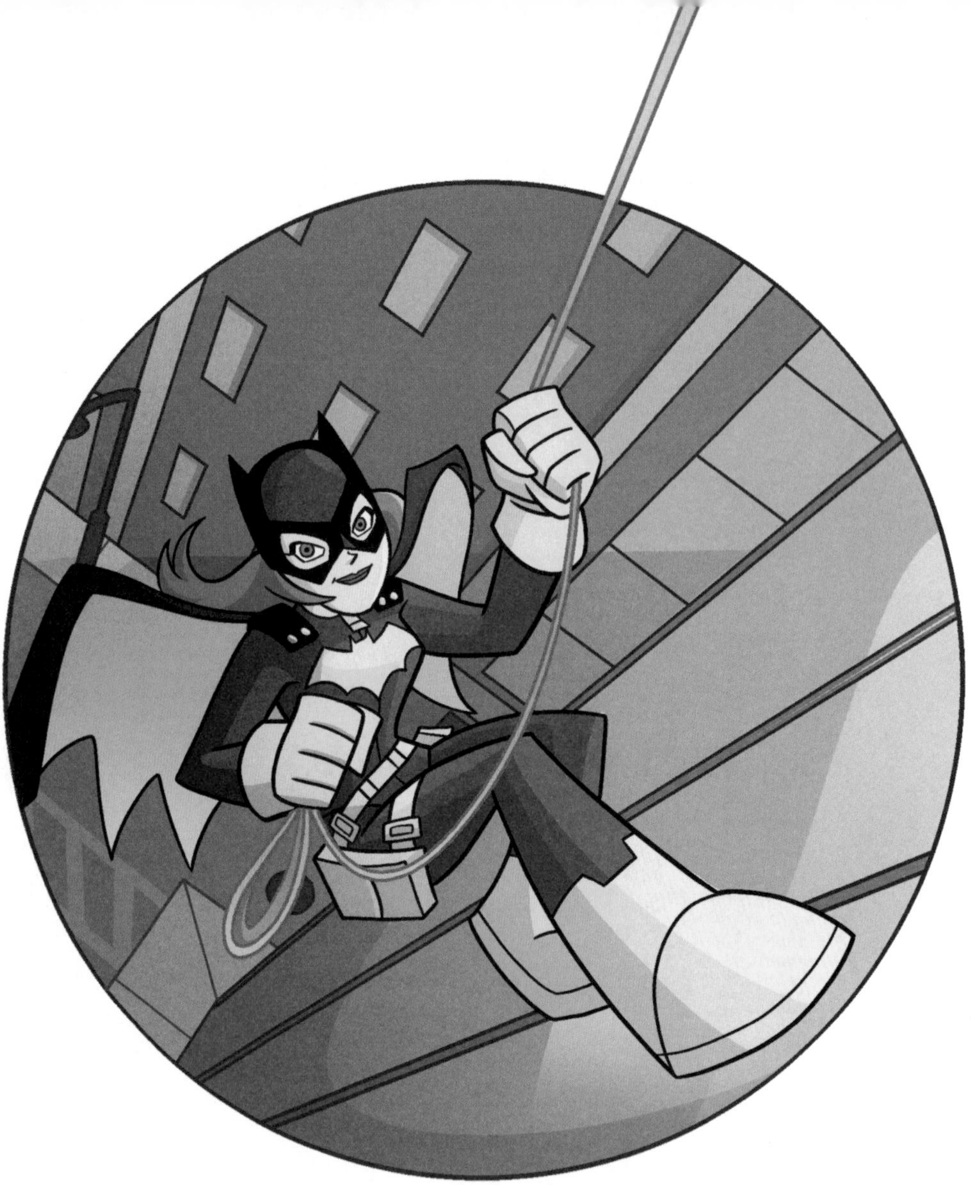

Batgirl is brave
and bold.

Bad guys, beware!

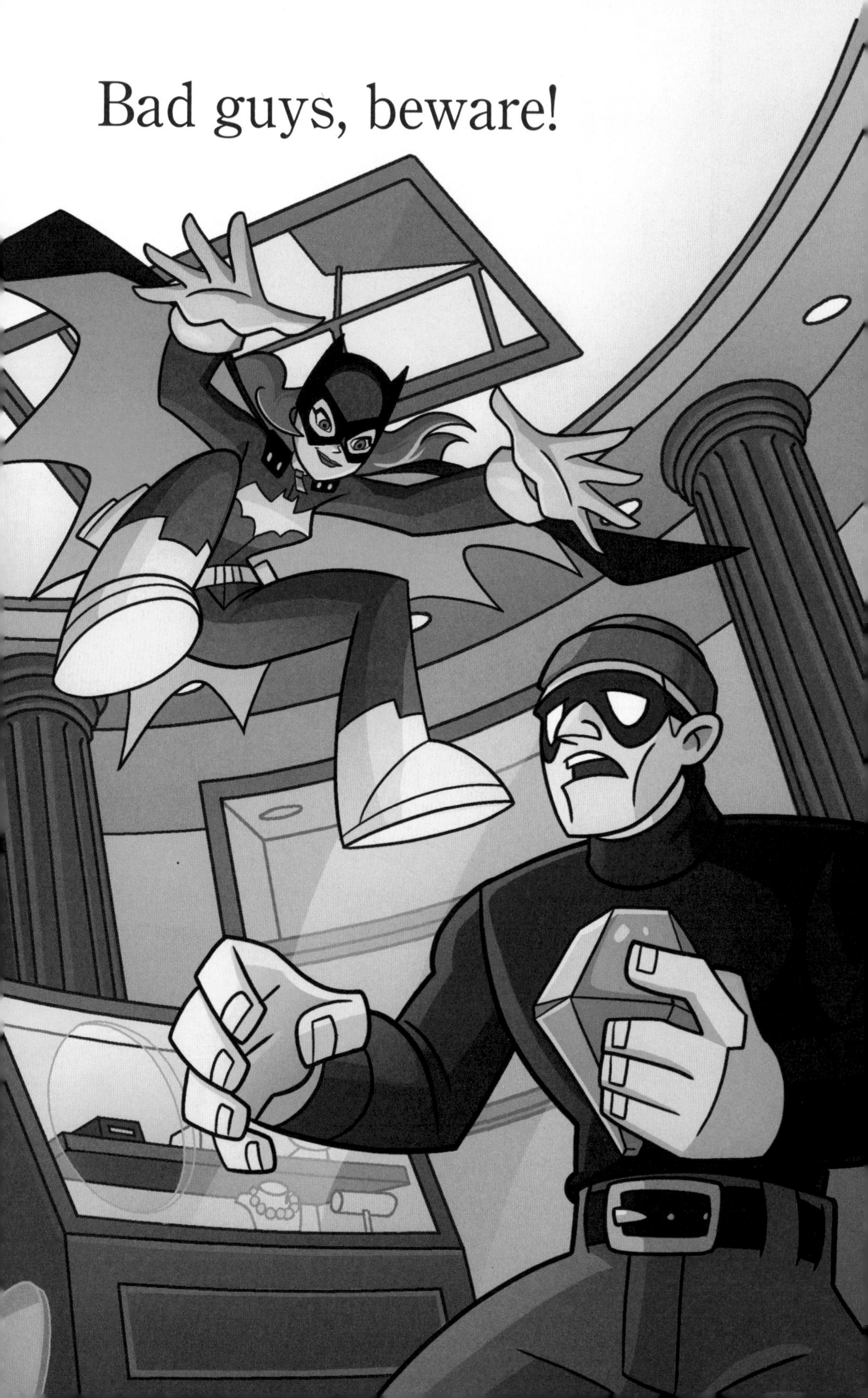

Nothing stops Batgirl
from saving the day!

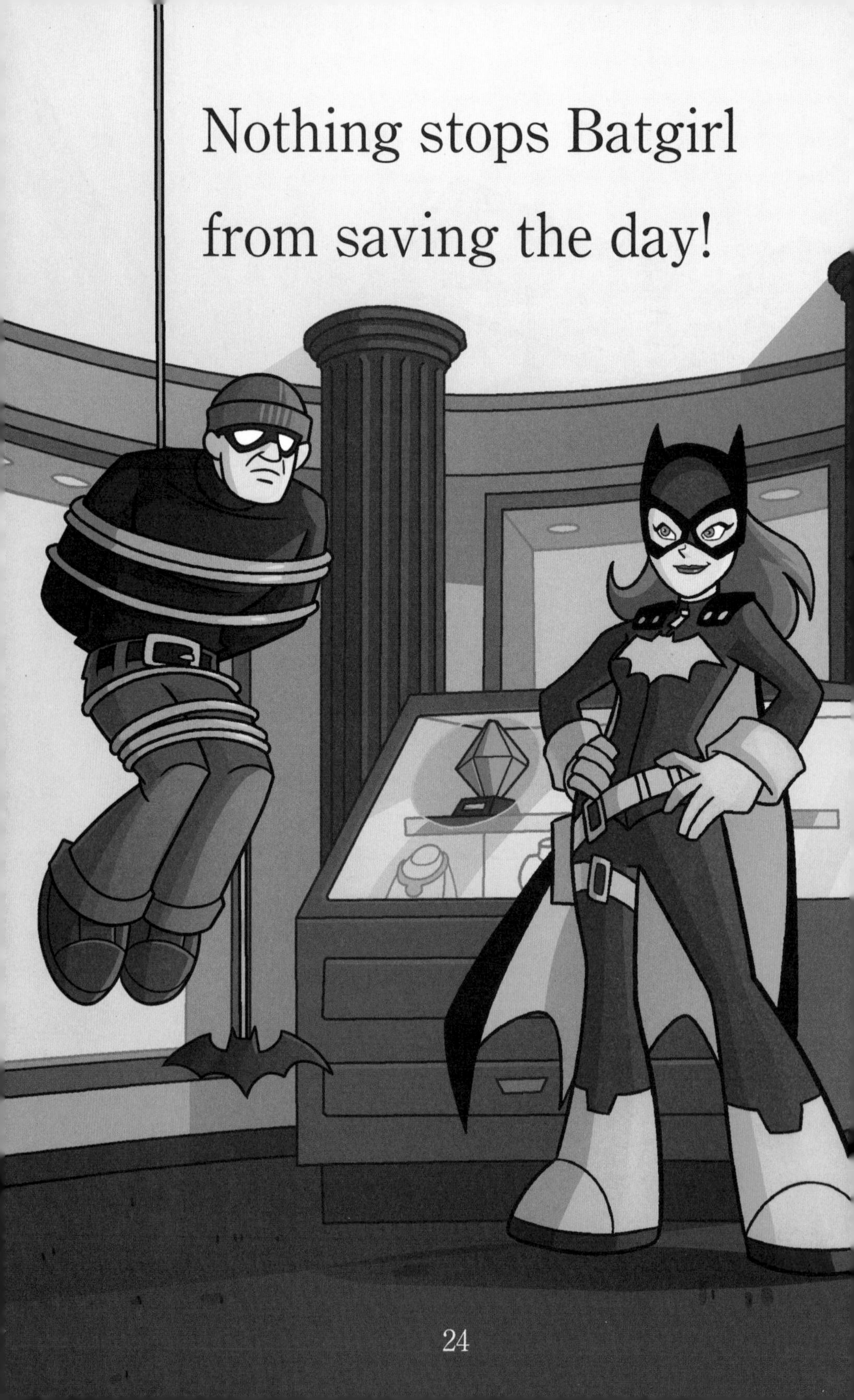

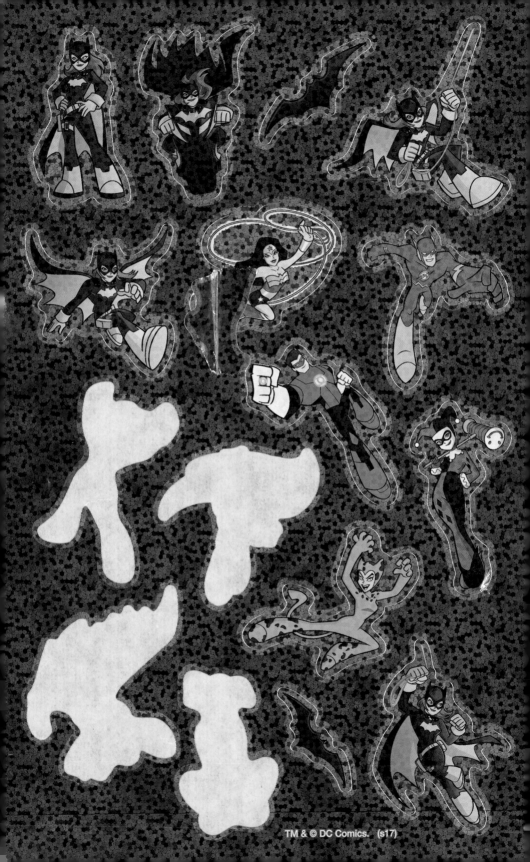

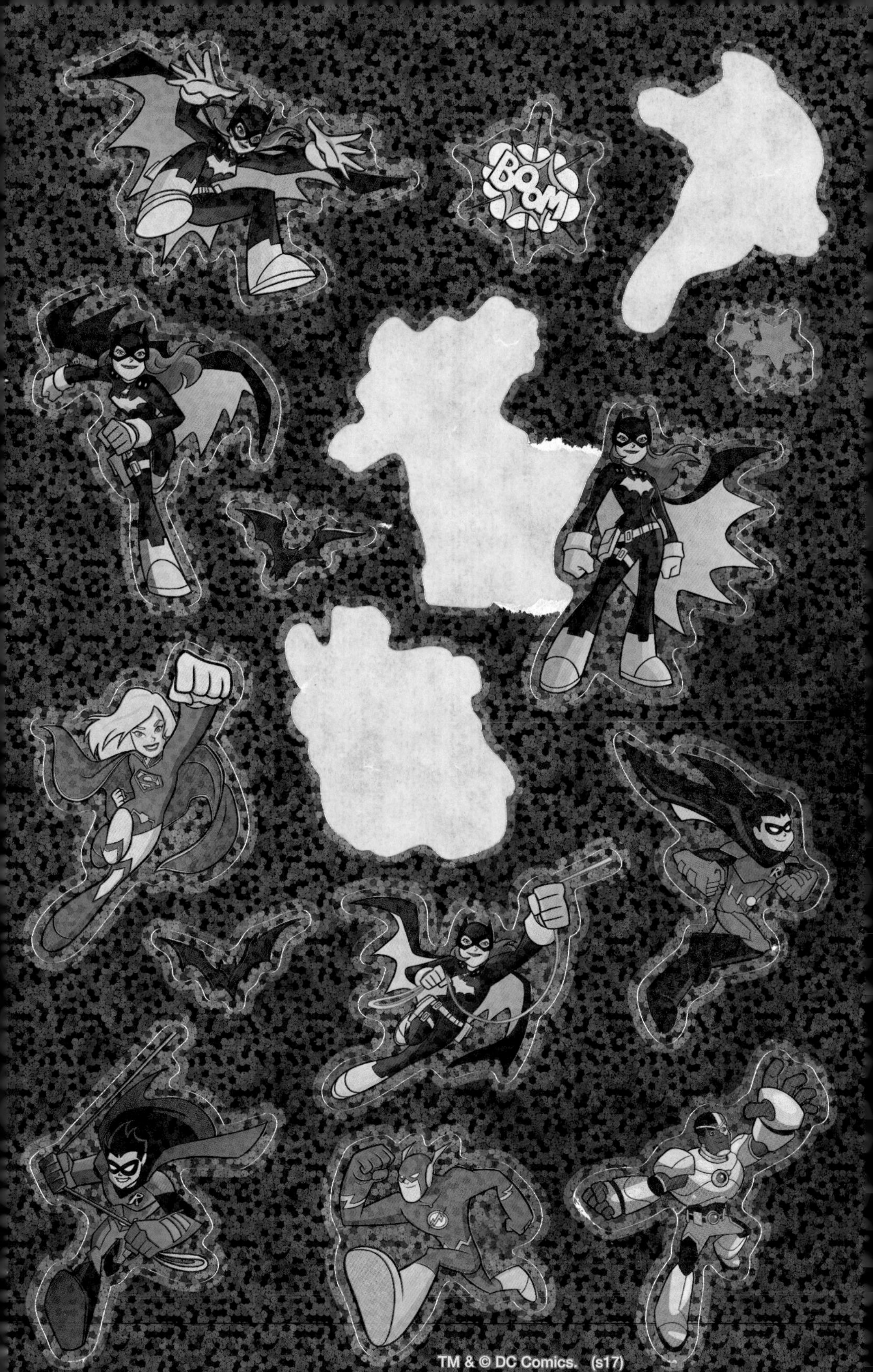
BOOM